MIA'S LIFE: FAN TAKEOVER!

Mia's Life
FAN TAKEOVER!

MIA FIZZ

sourcebooks
young readers

Published by Sourcebooks Young Readers, an imprint of Sourcebooks Kids
P.O. Box 4410, Naperville, Illinois 60567-4410
(630) 961-3900
sourcebookskids.com

Library of Congress Cataloging-in-Publication Data

Names: Fizz, Mia, author.
Title: Fan takeover! / Mia Fizz.
Description: Naperville, Illinois : Sourcebooks Young Readers, [2021] |
    Series: Mia's life ; 1 | Audience: Ages 7. | Audience: Grades 4-6. |
    Summary: "From Youtube sensation Mia Fizz comes a funny and charming
    illustrated series starter for tweens about gaining confidence and
    taking risks"-- Provided by publisher.
Identifiers: LCCN 2020053487 (print) | LCCN 2020053488 (ebook)
Classification: LCC PZ7.1.F57365 Fan 2021 (print) | LCC PZ7.1.F57365
    (ebook) | DDC [Fic]--dc23
LC record available at https://lccn.loc.gov/2020053487
LC ebook record available at https://lccn.loc.gov/2020053488

Source of Production: Versa Press, East Peoria, Illinois, United States
Date of Production: January 2021
Run Number: 5020631

Printed and bound in the United States of America.
VP 10 9 8 7 6 5 4 3 2 1

"Hey, Miacorns! Welcome back to *Mia's Life!*"

I said those words to begin every YouTube video on my channel, but they never got old.

"As you can see, today, I'm barefaced, and I'm going to show you the new toner that's been *so* incredible for my skin," I explained to the camera, holding up a hot-pink bottle. When I was making videos, it was easy to forget that more than one million people subscribed to my channel. Instead, it felt like it was just me, playing with makeup and talking about things I loved. That's really how *Mia's Life* started—I'd always loved sharing about my life! But now, I had a pretty popular YouTube channel. Okay...more like *super* popular. My videos weren't just seen by my family, but by people all over the world. It was my very own show, where I could show my life and talk about things average girls go through.

Like acne. *Ugh!*

I was just about to tell my viewers (a.k.a. the Miacorns!) why vitamin B3 is so important for your skincare routine when my phone buzzed with a reminder.

> Find Sienna's bday present—ASAP!

I groaned, leaning over and flicking off the camera. Toner and foundation would have to wait. My little sister, Sienna, was going to be nine years old in just five days. And I still didn't have a gift for her!

I took out my favorite journal and tapped my pencil, trying to get my creative juices flowing. Staring through the huge window in my room overlooking the backyard usually helped me get imaginative.

Things Sienna loved: Karma and Koa, our little sister and brother. Space. Vegan ice cream. Wonder Woman. Being in videos with me.

So maybe, like...a picture of all of us dressed like astronauts while we ate ice cream?

Ugh. I was drawing a complete blank.

Mom poked her head into my room. "Hey, sweetheart. Still filming?"

Some parents would probably be weirded out by their kid making videos for millions of people, but not mine. Mom and Dad loved that I made videos—in fact, sometimes we made them all together! They were super supportive, especially because I was learning a ton about owning a small business and internet safety. Mom helped me brainstorm videos all the time, while Dad helped manage a lot of my sponsor deals.

I shook my head. "No. I'm trying to think of ideas for Sienna's birthday present."

"Hmm. Any good ideas?"

"Um...homemade ice cream that's space-flavored?"

Mom wrinkled her nose. "What on earth is space-flavored? No pun intended."

I threw my hands in the air. "I don't know! I'm thinking out loud, here! What about a new shirt or something? A *Wonder Woman* one? Is that too dorky?"

Mom shrugged. "Well, you'd better hurry. You only have five days."

"Don't remind me," I grumbled.

Down the hall, Koa started crying. He was only six months old and needed a ton of attention. Sometimes it could be frustrating to be woken up in the middle of the night, but I loved having a tiny baby around. He was cute, squishy, and the ultimate pick-me-up.

"Somebody needs to be held," Mom said. "Keep brainstorming. You'll think of something."

I knew she was right, but I still felt a lot of pressure. I couldn't believe Sienna was going to be nine! Besides, we'd probably film her entire birthday morning. That meant millions of people would be watching her open whatever gift I gave her. What if she hated it? Or what if she didn't know what it was? Or what if—

My phone buzzed again, and I glanced at it. It was a text from my best friend, Briony. I didn't get to see her very much anymore, since I started homeschooling this year. Our family traveled a lot, and besides, I needed more time to work on my channel. Sometimes, I thought I learned more from *Mia's Life* than I did in school. I could spend a week in Portugal and learn about its history from museums and tour guides, or even study art by seeing the *Mona Lisa* in person.

> Hey! Mall tmr after school?? I really need new shoes. 👠

I quickly texted back.

As long as I get this video done at some point today! I just have my Spanish tutor in the afternoon but I'm free after 3. Can't wait xx

I loved hanging out with Briony. My brunette, freckle-faced bestie had known me before I was a YouTuber, and being with her made me feel completely normal. I was always myself on my channel, but there was still something special about being with someone who didn't care what kind of makeup I was wearing.

I still didn't have any ideas for Sienna's gift, but if I wanted to hang out with my BFF the next day, I had to get this tutorial done. I got back to my makeup, walking my followers through my vitamin supplements, foundation, and highlighter.

I knew my life wasn't exactly *normal*. Most girls just did their makeup in the bathroom or whatever, not for an audience. But being a YouTuber was my dream job. Some influencers only showed videos where they looked perfectly put-together with a full face of makeup. Not me. I loved knowing that showing off my real acne could help girls around the world with theirs. It made me feel so connected to people and like I was doing something that mattered. Sure, it was just makeup. But who doesn't feel more confident when they feel more beautiful? I also talked about things like puberty and my period and fights I had with my sister. I wanted the Miacorns to know that I really was a lot like them. It was my goal to help other girls in a way that felt approachable and fun. With *Mia's Life*, I could do exactly that.

After I finished the video, I sent the clips off to my editor. I knew that I should probably bank a few selfies for Instagram while I had a face full of makeup, but I wanted to get back to shopping for Sienna's birthday. I quickly brought up Pinterest and typed in *gifts for 9-year-old girls*.

"Can I borrow your blue sparkly headb— Hey, what are you doing?"

Oh no! It was Sienna!

"Nothing!" I closed the browser and shut my laptop as fast as I could.

"You were looking for birthday presents for me!" Sienna squealed excitedly.

"Was not."

"Was too!"

"Was *not!*"

"Girls! Please be kind!" Mom yelled from down the hall. I loved my sister, but we were still sisters, meaning sometimes we fought and drove each other up the wall.

"Yes, you can borrow the blue sparkly headband," I told Sienna. "It's in the bathroom, in the drawer with all the hair stuff."

"You're trying to distract me," said Sienna. "I *know* that's what you were doing! Mia, my birthday is in five days. If you order something today, it won't even come on time!"

"*Hello?* Two-day shipping," I said with a grin.

"*Mia!*"

"Sienna, relax. I've got it all taken care of."

"If you say so," she said suspiciously. "I'm gonna grab the headband."

While she walked into the bathroom, I quickly opened my laptop and shut down the browser windows I had open. Whew—that was a close one!

"How does it look?" asked Sienna as she came back into my room. She had the headband tugged over her head, but it was pushing her ears forward.

"Come here," I laughed, securing it in place for her. I pulled a few wispy hairs out in the front to make it look more natural before tossing her braid over her shoulder. "There. You look perfect. Are you doing pictures or something?" Sienna always had to do photos for Instagram with Mom or Dad, since she was only nine. They managed her page for her.

"I'm gonna do an Instagram later to show off my new shirt," she said, gesturing to the shirt she was wearing. It was a Wonder Woman shirt, complete with a sparkly gold W. Darn—there went that idea.

"Well, go do it, then. I have to brainstorm my next few videos."

"What do you have going up this week?" asked Sienna, sitting on my bed and flopping down onto my pillows. Welcome to life with three siblings—no personal space.

"A new makeup tutorial. How to cover up my bad acne I'm having this week," I said with an eye roll.

"Hmm."

Here's the other thing about sisters: you *always* know what they mean. That *hmm* could have meant a thousand things, like *Hmm, that's interesting* or *Hmm, I'm sure that will be helpful.*

But nope. That one meant *Hmm, that's totally boring.*

"What's wrong with makeup tutorials?" I asked.

"Nothing!" she said. "I just... I mean, you do a lot of them."

"They're popular," I reminded her. "People like makeup."

"That's true."

"And I got sent that new toner, and it's been working wonders on my face. Seriously. It's taken my skin from, like, Emergency Level to Moderately Manageable."

Sienna giggled.

"Do you think people are getting sick of them?" I asked worriedly. Sienna was my most loyal viewer. She was also great at tracking which videos were popular and which fell flat.

"Well, no..." She bit her nails a little, thinking. "I don't know. Maybe. You've just been doing so many of them recently. Like..." She flipped open my laptop and brought up my channel. My last five videos were:

Sephora MAKEUP HAUL! 📸

How I Do My EVERYDAY LOOK ✨

The best BACK-TO-SCHOOL makeup looks

How I Store my MAKEUP COLLECTION!

Transforming myself into a MERMAID w/ MAKEUP 🧜

"You may have a point," I admitted.

"I think you need to shake it up!" said Sienna, waving her hands in the air. "You know, do something...with a new vibe."

"A new vibe?" I asked skeptically.

"Yeah, something different. A prank video? We used to love making those."

"I don't know. They can be kind of mean. Or destructive," I said. One of my favorite YouTubers had just gotten in huge trouble for playing a prank on their parents that somehow ended with the microwave on fire.

"Let me think. What about a challenge or something?" my sister suggested. "Or wait, I know! A takeover!" She clapped her hands together in excitement. "A takeover would be *so* perfect for you!"

"A takeover?"

"Yeah, a *fan* takeover! Like, people who watch your videos will get to vote and make decisions for you. I've seen some other YouTubers do them, and they're always *so* funny."

"Maybe," I said thoughtfully.

"You're the vlogger. You can figure it out. I just think mixing it up might be good," she responded with a shrug.

"Knock knock." It was Dad, standing in my doorway, my two-year-old sister Karma sitting on his shoulders. "Who wants to take a break and help their poor dad make dinner?"

"Me!" shouted Sienna.

"It's-a pizza time," Dad said in an exaggerated Italian accent. He kissed his fingers like a chef. Dad was always such a goofball—it made him a perfect fit for YouTube!

"Did you get the good cheese?" I asked.

"You know it," he promised. By the good cheese, I meant the vegan cheese that *didn't* taste like the inside of an old shoe. My family had been eating vegan for more than seven years, ever since we saw a documentary on how beneficial it was for the planet. These days, I honestly liked vegan alternatives way more than meat or dairy.

"Maybe I should film it," I said. "Sienna thinks my channel is getting boring."

"I didn't say *boring!*" she protested. "I said that you could mix it up."

"You have been doing a lot of makeup videos lately," Dad pointed out.

"*Dad!* You too? Was nobody going to tell me before this that I was on the edge of becoming totally mind-numbingly dull?" I cried.

"Toe-tawy!" Karma shrieked. I glared right at her, the two-year-old traitor. But as soon as she stuck her tongue out at me, we all couldn't help but crack up.

"Come on, Family Fizz," Dad said. "Let's go make some magic happen in the kitchen."

"I'll be right there," I promised.

Dad turned out of my room with Karma, and Sienna followed them. I sat and stared at my camera.

Was I really turning, as Karma said, toe-tawy dull? My makeup videos still got a ton of views. My fans always sent me DMs on Instagram about how much they loved them.

But maybe Sienna was right. And lately, when I'd been prepping and filming my makeup videos, I'd had a hard time concentrating. Even *I* felt a little tired of them.

Great. Now I had to find my sister the perfect birthday present *and* find a way to "mix it up" on my channel.

Being a YouTuber wasn't easy!

That night, after Sienna had gone to bed, I sat at the table and pulled my laptop out. I'd decided she was right. A fan takeover did sound sort of fun.

"What are you working on?" Mom asked as she came downstairs from putting down Koa in the nursery.

"Mom, do you think my channel is getting...stale?" I asked.

"Stale? No way!" Mom said, pulling down a chair and plopping down next to me at the table. "Your subscribers have been steadily increasing, and your ad revenue is... Well, let's just say that when you want to do your around-the-world trip, it's not going to be an issue." See what I told you? Supportive.

"I hope you're right."

"Did you get a mean DM?" Mom asked worriedly. I didn't have a ton of interaction with haters. My Instagram fans could send me direct messages, but I usually didn't reply; I preferred to comment on posts publicly, so things were out in the open. And YouTube didn't allow comments on my videos since I wasn't eighteen years old.

"No," I said. "Sienna and Dad just pointed out how many of my videos have to do with makeup. Sienna suggested maybe doing a fan takeover. I thought that sounded pretty fun."

Mom nodded thoughtfully. "This calls for ice cream. Strategy session in three minutes. Bring comfy pants that stretch."

I laughed before heading into my room to change into cozy sweats.

When I came back to the dining room, there were two huge bowls of vegan chocolate ice cream on the table (*yum!*) and mom was scribbling in a notebook.

"What are you writing?" I asked.

"I'm trying to come up with some ideas for Sienna's party this weekend," Mom said. "I found these galaxy-themed vegan cake pops we can order. And I really want to get one of those over-the-top balloon garlands...but do we have to blow those up ourselves?"

"Good question. If we did, we'd probably pass out." I giggled and took a bite of ice cream.

"I also had an idea for a photo booth. We could get some geolocation, so people could add a sticker to their stories saying they were at the party."

"Love that," I said. "Hashtag SiennaTurnsNine?"

"Perfect!" said Mom. "I'll call tomorrow. We need to start planning these nitty-gritty details. The party's this weekend!"

"Maybe I could film it for one of my videos," I mused. "That would be mixing it up."

"What was the fan takeover idea Sienna was talking about? That sounded interesting," Mom replied.

I explained to her what a takeover was. Basically, it meant presenting my followers with polls they could vote on for a day, like what color clothes I would wear or where I would go. Letting them really decide my day. Some of the takeovers Sienna had me watch were absolutely nuts—one vlogger's fans even sent her on a helicopter ride!

Mom laughed. "I love it! You're always talking about wanting to connect with your fans. This sounds like the perfect way to do it, don't you think?"

Mom had a point. I was always trying to find ways to make my fans feel close to me. I didn't want to be one of those vloggers who seemed like an unapproachable celebrity. That just totally wasn't me! I wanted my fans to feel like they were my friends. In a way, they were. Some kids probably spent too much time online, but one of my favorite parts of the internet was the way you could make friends across the globe. Briony helped me choose what to wear and what to do. Why couldn't the Miacorns?

"Okay," I agreed. "But what could we let them pick between?"

"Hmm," said Mom thoughtfully. "Something low-key to start with, probably. Just to see how it goes."

"Maybe an outfit?"

"What about something with makeup?" Mom said. "I know you were worried your makeup videos were getting stale, but think of it this way: The Miacorns are used to seeing you do makeup videos. It would be on brand, talking about something you love, *and* a way to mix it up."

"Okay. Like, picking an eyeshadow color?" I said thoughtfully.

"Maybe something more dramatic." Mom took our now-empty bowls to the sink and started rinsing them out. "What about...a couple of out-there looks? To wear out in public?"

"What do you mean?" I asked.

"Hmm." Mom pulled out her phone and sat back

down at the table, and I scooted my chair close to her as we surfed Pinterest.

"Unicorn sparkles? Like Miacorns, get it?" Mom asked.

"Umm...I've already done a couple different unicorn looks."

"What about this?" Mom pulled up a photo of a model at a fashion show with a colorful rhinestone-eye look. It was bright blue and shimmery, making her look completely cool for the runway. But completely out there for me—definitely not my usual everyday look!

"Wow. It's definitely wild," I agreed.

"Maybe you could let your viewers choose either this look or no makeup at all," said Mom. "And you could walk around the mall."

I gulped. Neither of those sounded great to me! I liked to play with makeup now and then on my channel, but not in public. Doing things for the Miacorns was one thing. Doing it here, in my hometown, where real, live people would see me? The thought of going out to the mall with no makeup sounded terrifying—my acne had really been flaring up lately. But the thought of going with that out-there rhinestone look was just as scary!

"Um..."

"Mia," Mom said patiently, picking up on my hesitation. "How are you going to shake things up if you're afraid to get out of your comfort zone?"

"I guess you're right," I said nervously. "I *am* supposed to go to the mall with Briony tomorrow."

"So, post a poll! What's the worst that could happen?"

I quickly snapped a selfie before I could change my mind, followed by the rhinestone eye look and an earlier photo of me barefaced. I quickly used an app to photoshop

WHICH ONE?

Ⓐ rhinestone eyes

Ⓑ makeup-free

all three together, side by side. Then I uploaded it to Instagram with the poll.

"It's just makeup, Mia. It's for fun," Mom reminded me. "It could be a great example for your followers. About being yourself and taking risks, without being too self-conscious."

"How'd you get so smart?" I asked with a grin.

"It's a mom thing," she said. "And speaking of mom things, it's time for bed, isn't it? You need your beauty sleep if you're going to let your fans take over your day tomorrow!"

It wasn't until I was curled up under my bright pink comforter that I realized we hadn't solved my other problem—Sienna's birthday present. *Oh, well*, I thought. *Maybe I can get something at the mall...no matter what my face looks like!*

The next morning, my alarm went off, but I reached over and hit Snooze. Perk of homeschooling—if I wanted to have a bit of a slow, lazy morning, Mom and Dad didn't mind as long as I got my schoolwork done. I hadn't been able to sleep—I kept brainstorming ideas for Sienna's birthday present. Here's what I came up with:

Yes, you read that correctly.

Nothing. Nada. Zip.

I heard the rest of my family clattering around noisily in the kitchen, which made it hard to fall back asleep.

I dragged myself out of bed, yanking on my favorite fuzzy sweater. I could hear Mom singing the ABCs with Karma and Dad reminding Sienna to brush her teeth.

"Good morning, sunshine!" Dad said as I came into the kitchen. "Coconut yogurt?"

"Ooh, yummy. Thanks." I grabbed the cup he was holding out. "Passion fruit?"

"Your favorite," he confirmed.

"Mia, Mom told me you're doing my takeover idea!" Sienna said excitedly. "Did you check the poll yet?"

The Instagram poll! How had I forgotten? I whipped out my phone and brought up the poll. I had a ton of DMs, but I went straight to the poll results.

It wasn't even close. *Gulp*. Ten percent of people wanted me to go barefaced...while a whopping ninety percent of voters were hoping for the rhinestone eye look.

"I guess I'd better get out my craft supplies," I said, showing Sienna the photo.

"You're going to look *so* rad," Sienna said. "That's the one I voted for too."

I rolled my eyes. "You're not supposed to vote!"

"Says who?"

"Sienna, we're going to be late for your tutoring session. Grab your bag and get a move on," Dad said.

I yanked on Sienna's messy bun. "Have a good day."

"You too! Bye! And take a million pictures of the makeup. I can't wait to see it!"

Sienna was only one person, but when she and Dad left, the volume in the house fell dramatically. It almost felt peaceful for a second, before Koa whacked Karma with his bottle and she burst into tears. You could always count on a house full of siblings to be loud.

"What's on the agenda for today?" Mom asked, trying to calm Karma down. She looked tired—Koa had been up quite a few times in the night.

"Well, this morning I have to reply to some Instagram comments. Then I was going to work out to get a little PE in, and work on *Jane Eyre*," I said. My homeschool curriculum was very individualized. I got to pick whatever classics I wanted to read for English class, and gym consisted of me doing weights or going on a walk instead of playing basketball in a sweaty gymnasium. Fitness was really important to my family—Mom and Dad were all about making sure we stayed as healthy as possible.

"Don't forget that you have Spanish this afternoon," Mom said.

"I won't." Spanish was my favorite subject. I wanted to become completely fluent one day. I'd even done a few fun YouTube videos where I only spoke in Spanish to my family; they were super popular. Suddenly, a thought occurred to me. I struck my forehead with my palm. "Oh no! I'm leaving for the mall with Briony right after Spanish!"

"So?"

"*So?* I've got to do my rhinestone eye first since I won't

have time after. That means I'm going to have to wear that makeup for my video call with Señorita Gomez!"

Mom cracked up. "Well, I'm sure it will be muy bonita."

Two chapters of *Jane Eyre* and one refreshing workout later, I got to work. I pulled out my favorite eyeshadow palette a brand had sent me a few months ago, my liquid eyeliner, some glitter spray, and the family's craft bucket. At the bottom of the bucket, I found a few silver rhinestones rolling around. Perfect!

I started by blending a few different shades of blue eyeshadow onto my eyelids, starting with lighter colors and shifting toward a more oceanic navy. Then, I did a silver cat eye, extending the eyeshadow about an inch away from my actual eyelid. I lined the whole thing with black liner and dotted it with a few rhinestones, placing them carefully, since I knew they'd be a pain to redo. I sprayed all of it with some turquoise glitter spray.

It looked pretty good, if I did say so myself!

At least, it looked like the photo. It definitely wasn't what I would wear for an ordinary trip to the mall.

Doing my makeup for the camera always took a little longer, since I paused to explain things to the Miacorns and show off the exact products I was using, and I had to send the clips off to our editor. By the time I was done, it was just about time for Spanish.

"Wow, Mia! It looks terrific," Mom said, poking her head in my room.

"Thanks," I said, trying to see it from different angles in my makeup mirror. "It's definitely...shaking things up."

"I can't wait to hear about people's reactions. It's going to be an awesome video," she said.

My computer started chiming with the familiar Skype ringtone. "Adios, mama. I have class."

"I'm putting Koa down for a nap. Come out after, and we'll take some pictures."

When Señorita Gomez popped up on the screen, her jaw dropped. I sighed.

"How do you say *life of a Youtuber* in Spanish?"

The doorbell rang, and I raced to get it. I had finally gotten all of my verbs right, and now I could finally get to buying Sienna her birthday gift!

"Hey!" I said, flinging open the door. "Ready to go?" I threw a handful of dry cereal into my mouth. It was one of my favorite snacks.

"Um...did you forget to tell me something?" she said, pointing to my face.

"Sorry—want some cereal?"

"No, Mia! Your makeup!"

"What?" I glanced in the hallway mirror. Oh, yeah. The bright blue rhinestone eye. "Well...we may have to do a bit of filming at the mall. Sorry."

She laughed. "I saw your poll last night. I voted rhinestone. I can't believe how good it looks!"

I grinned. "It took me *forever*. I just hope people don't get weirded out."

"Isn't the point for people to be weirded out?" she asked. "Oh, my gosh, Koa! He's getting huge!" My baby brother was gleefully babbling at us. I leaned down and scooped him up. Karma was trotting along behind him.

"Blue," she informed Briony, pointing to my face.

"Good job, Karma! That's right!" I cooed.

"You girls have fun," Mom yelled from the kitchen. "And be careful!"

"We will," we yelled back, plopping my siblings on the couch and heading out the door to Briony's mom's car. Our next-door neighbor, Mrs. Granger, held up her hand to wave but froze when she saw my face.

Oh, boy. Was this going to be what the whole afternoon was like?

5

As soon as we pulled up to the mall, I got my answer: yes, that was what the whole afternoon was going to be like!

Briony and I walked into the food court together after her mom dropped us off. My best friend was like me: she liked to keep her makeup and clothes fun, but pretty natural. So all of the people looking at us wasn't at all what we were used to.

I handed Briony the camera I use to film videos, complete with a little handheld stand so she could get a good angle. "You're the best. Thanks for doing this."

"I'm used to it," she said with a grin. "Most kids our age work at, like, Starbucks. But *my* best friend glues

glitter and rhinestones to her face and films what people think." We giggled.

Speaking of Starbucks, it was definitely going to be our first stop! Briony loved Frappuccinos, and I always got an almond milk iced latte.

"Hi," I said cheerfully to the barista.

"Um...hi. What can I get you?" The guy looked a couple years older than us, and he was totally confused. Briony started giggling.

"A grande iced almond milk latte and a grande chocolate chip Frappuccino, please."

"Okay...um...let me just...ring that up."

"Thanks," I said with a grin. After we paid for our drinks, Briony asked through her giggles if he minded if we shared the video on YouTube. If he had said no, we would have blurred his face out—it was important for me not to put people on the internet who didn't want to be there.

"You're a vlogger? That's really cool," he said. "And,

hey, I like the look! I was just a little surprised. It's cool how bold it is."

"Thanks," I said. Maybe Mom was right—sometimes, stepping out of your makeup comfort zone can work wonders on your confidence! I was already feeling like this trip to the mall was more fun than usual.

Next, after we grabbed our drinks, we walked toward Briony's favorite store to get her some new ballet flats. As we strolled, I noticed a lot of people doing double takes. The rhinestone eye definitely stood out! But instead of feeling awkward, I was actually feeling pretty good. What's so bad about attracting a little attention? I had a colorful personality, and now, I had the makeup to match it!

"Plain or patterned?" Briony asked, holding up a pair of white flats next to a pair of leopard-print ones. Best Foot Forward was where we got all of our shoes. Their selection was ginormous.

"Hmm," I said, considering the options. "I like them both—"

"Wow! Your makeup is incredible," a girl shopping for flip-flops interrupted. She looked right around our age and was with someone who must have been her mom. "I love it. Did you watch a YouTube video to get it right?"

"Sort of," I said, before turning to wink at the camera. Ha! The Miacorns would love that!

"You don't look like someone who would like plain shoes," she said. "I love the leopard ones, personally!"

"They're actually for my friend, but I agree," I told the girl. I turned to Briony. "Leopard?"

"Leopard it is!" she said.

After making sure they had the leopard flats in her size, we went up to the register. The salesclerk was an older woman, maybe a little older than my mom.

"Hmm," she sniffed as she checked us out. Oops... She definitely wasn't into the rhinestone eye! "I see you're getting a lot of attention."

I giggled nervously. Well, duh! You don't wear bright-blue sparkly makeup to blend in!

"Please put that camera away," she snapped at Briony, who quickly lowered it.

"No problem," I assured her. She handed Briony her new shoes and we left in a hurry, arm in arm. She watched us go, as if blue eyeshadow meant we would suddenly try to sneak ballet flats out in our purses without paying. Jeez!

"Well, *she* wasn't very polite," said Briony.

"Not everybody likes to be filmed," I reminded her.

"She didn't have to be a jerk about it, though! I see you're getting a lot of *attention*," mimicked Briony, which made me laugh.

"Come on," I said, throwing my arm around her. "Let's have fun and not worry about haters."

"At least I got my shoes," she said, pulling them out of the bag. "They're cute, don't you think?"

"Adorable."

"Everyone at school has been really into ballet flats lately," Briony explained. That was good to know. It was helpful having a best friend go to regular school;

she could help me stay on top of the trends, which was really helpful for my videos! It could be tricky to balance having a typical life and, well...not having one at all. I knew most girls my age weren't homeschooled YouTubers who got to travel the world with their family on a regular basis, and I understood how privileged I was to have that opportunity. But that didn't mean I didn't have all the same insecurities other girls did.

"Should we make an Instagram story, or do you want to save it for your video?" asked Briony.

"Let's save it," I said. "I want to do a big reveal, not spoil it with some short-term content."

Briony laughed. "You sound so professional!"

"It *is* my job," I reminded her.

"Yeah, well, it doesn't always feel like work," she teased.

"Hey," I said with a grin, "I said it was my job, not that it wasn't super fun!"

"Well, *I* say we grab some soft pretzels," Briony said. "All of that shoe-picking was exhausting."

"Only if you promise to help me think of a birthday present for Sienna. I'm running out of time!"

"Deal."

We swung by the pretzel stand, and I was happy to see they'd recently added a vegan cheese option. Yum! The pretzel clerk complimented my look and asked where I got the eyeshadow. She was definitely a lot nicer than the shoe salesperson. We chatted about makeup for a minute while she heated up our pretzels and took our cash. But Briony and I had just found a bench and taken the first bite of steaming-hot pretzel when I heard someone say—

"Mia? Oh, my gosh, is that you?"

I'd been spotted!

Now, I'm not an A-list celebrity. It's not like I can't do things like go to the mall or grab a soft pretzel. But when I'm somewhere a lot of kids my own age hang out—like the mall—chances are pretty high I'm going to run into a Miacorn.

Or an entire herd of them.

"Hi," I said to the girls who spoke to me.

"Oh, my gosh!" The two girls squealed together. One had a long side ponytail, and one had her red hair piled into two knots on her head.

I just laughed. "It's nice to meet you. What are your names?"

"I'm April," the girl with the braids said, "and this is Rory. We're, like—"

"Your biggest fans ever!" Rory exclaimed. "Your makeup... Oh my gosh! The poll! We both voted!"

April nodded. "We thought the rhinestone eye would look amazing. It's so different from your everyday look! Not that there's anything wrong with your usual look, *obvi*. It's just..."

"Good to mix it up every now and then," I finished for her.

"Exactly," they said in unison.

Briony took a big bite of pretzel and flipped through her phone. Some friends may have been weirded out by their BFF getting recognized in public, but she was pretty used to it.

"Can we get a picture with you?" asked Rory.

"Totally," I said.

"I'll take it!" Briony offered cheerfully, putting her phone down and picking up my camera.

"Oh, my gosh, are we going to be *in* a video?" asked April. "Like, a real *Mia's Life* video?!"

Briony laughed. "Sure. Just tell the camera what you think of her look!"

"We love it!" they shouted.

"Wait, is that—are you—" Another girl suddenly ran up to us.

"Mia Fizz!" Now *another* girl from another direction was hurrying over, snapping pictures with her phone.

Oh, boy.

Briony and I spent the next forty-five minutes taking photos, interviewing girls about how they liked the rhinestone eye makeup, and signing autographs. My hand was starting to cramp up! Some girls had me sign receipts or random scraps of paper, but one girl actually asked me to scrawl my name across the back of her hand.

"This is the coolest day of my life," she told me. "I begged my mom to let me go shopping today, and she almost said no! Wait until I tell her Mia Fizz was here!"

Another girl had me sign her backpack with a Sharpie while her mom told me how she had stayed up so late watching my videos the night before that she had gotten in trouble.

"Mom," the girl groaned. "Play it cool."

"No worries," I said, smiling. "My mom would say the exact same thing!"

"I know she would," said the girl with a smile. "That's why I love your videos so much. It's like, you totally get me. You get how moms can be kind of pushy and sisters can be kind of annoying, but you still love your family so much, and it's just...inspiring."

"Same here," a brunette girl with glasses said. "And I've always been super into colorful makeup, but I was too chicken to wear it anywhere but my house. I'm totally going to rock this look to school next week. I mean, if you can do it, so can I!"

I felt like the Grinch when his heart grew three sizes. This was exactly why I poured so much time into *Mia's Life*. I wanted girls just like these to feel understood.

"Mia, did you look at the time?" Briony asked suddenly. "It's five thirty-five! I have, like, eight texts from my mom. She's outside."

"Oh no!" I cried. "I didn't get a chance to grab Sienna a birthday present! I didn't even think of what to get her."

"Uh-oh! Isn't her birthday party this week?" one of my fans asked. "I saw her post about it on Instagram. She's so cute!"

"Saturday," I groaned. "And it's already Wednesday! I'm almost out of time." Then, I had a brilliant idea. "Wait a second, you guys watch our videos! You know Sienna just as well as anyone. Do any of you have ideas for her birthday present?"

The girls all looked at one another before shrugging.

"Well, it was worth a shot," I grumbled.

"Don't worry," a tall girl with tons of freckles said. "You'll think of the perfect gift! After all, you're Mia Fizz. Whatever you pick is going to be *super* cool."

The other girls all agreed, but I had a sinking feeling in my stomach. All of these girls looked up to me *so* much. It was like every decision I made had to be the right one. I wanted to be a great sister to Sienna—and I wanted to be an example for big sisters everywhere. But I was seriously starting to panic. I had four days to find Sienna's present, and not a single idea.

"You'll know it when you see it," Briony assured me as we walked out to her mom's car. I just hoped she was right.

While Sienna was up in her room doing schoolwork, Mom and I spent the next morning organizing the decorations she'd picked up for Sienna's space party. She'd had an amazing banner printed, covered with sparkly stars. It said *Happy Birthday Sienna* in a curly-swirly script. She was going to love it!

Dad walked in. "So," he said, "how did the big fan takeover go?"

"Great!" I told him all about it, from the Starbucks barista to the spontaneous fan gathering.

"Wow! Sounds like it was a success," said Dad. "What are you going to do next?"

"Next?"

"Yeah, next!" He opened up the fridge and grabbed a bag of grapes. "If the fan takeover got great engagement, why not do another?"

I shrugged. "Good point. It could be fun to do another one."

Dad popped a few grapes in his mouth before snatching a piece of paper from the stack of mail that had been sitting on the counter. "I have the perfect idea. Everyone knows you're not exactly, well...coordinated."

"Okay, ouch!" It was totally true, though. I was known in my family for being a total klutz! There were a ton of videos where I fell, ran into things, and dropped stuff. I didn't mind—it was just who I was! Besides, it usually made people laugh.

"So...look. Here's the youth center flyer." Dad held the paper out to me. "They have all these different classes you could take! Rock climbing, dancing—"

"Dancing?" I froze. That sounded like my worst nightmare!

"Facing your fears," said Mom, pointing her coffee cup at me. "Another great lesson for the Miacorns." Darn—Mom always knew how to get to me.

I covered my face. "Fine. But everyone cross your fingers. If I have to take a dance class, it's going to be the most humiliating video I've ever done."

"Maybe Briony would take it with you," laughed Mom.

I snapped a photo of the flyer for the fan takeover. Karma started singing the ABCs as Koa giggled at her.

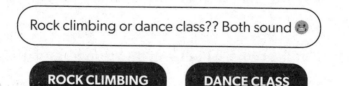

"All right! It's posted." I grabbed my water bottle and took a long swig. "Now, to see if I have to embarrass myself by falling off a cliff or attempting to do a pirouette."

"I don't think the youth center has actual cliffs," Dad pointed out.

"Doesn't make me feel any better," I retorted.

"By the way, did you grab your sister a present at the mall yesterday?" Mom asked.

"Um...about that."

"Mia Fizz! You can't be serious. Her birthday is in two days!"

"I know!" I buried my face in my hands. "But I just can't think of anything. What did you get her? Can't I just, I don't know, say it's from me too?"

"Sienna's not just your sister. She's one of your best friends," Mom said as she tied Karma's hair back in a ponytail. "I don't think that would make her feel good."

I sighed. "I've just had so much on my mind lately. Trying to shake things up for the channel, studying for Spanish...I feel totally fried, like my brain isn't working."

"Well, maybe some physical activity will you do you good, then," said Dad, waving the flyer in my face.

"Maybe," I said, as I grabbed it from him. "If it doesn't make me break a leg."

"Mia!"

It was Sienna, bursting into my bedroom. I had just finished uploading my rhinestone eye video. I'd spent all morning painting a welcome sign for Sienna's birthday party—my form of art class. It was draped out to dry on our back patio. The decorations were going to be perfect, and so was the food! The vegan moon-and-stars cake pops Mom had ordered looked beautiful.

"Dad says to get your shoes on," she said, grinning. "You're leaving for the youth center in ten minutes."

"What?"

She held out her phone. There it was: my poll.

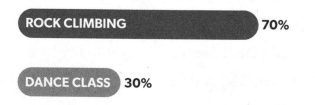

On one hand, thank goodness—the last thing I wanted to do was go to a dance class! But on the other hand...rock climbing? Me? I definitely wasn't what people would call athletic!

"Great," I groaned.

"It'll be fun," she said. "The beginner class is this afternoon, so it's perfect. They still had a spot available, so Dad claimed it for you."

"Are you coming?"

"No. Mom and I are going to take Karma to her baby gymnastics class."

"So you get to watch a ton of adorable toddlers do somersaults, and I have to go climb a wall and probably humiliate myself for a million people?"

"Yup," she said cheerfully. "But Dad will be there!"

I reached over to flick her topknot, but she was already running out the door.

Ugh. I so did not want to do this. But then I remembered those girls at the mall, telling me that my confidence to rock such an out-of-this-world makeup look gave them the confidence to do the same thing. What if somewhere, there was a clumsy Miacorn who had a dream of trying rock climbing? And what if seeing my video made her feel brave? Or any viewer who wanted to try something outside their comfort zone but felt scared. It didn't have to be rock climbing. It was all about taking a risk and putting yourself out there.

I could do this.

Where were my tennis shoes? Is that what people even wore rock climbing? If it was going to be for a video, I had to look halfway decent, but if I wore a bunch of makeup to a rock-climbing class, wouldn't that be weird? Oh, well. I quickly rubbed on just a touch of foundation and some lip gloss. Having a fresh face on made me feel more confident. If people at the class thought that was bizarre, I didn't care. Too bad I didn't have time for my rhinestone eyes!

"Hurry up, Mia!" Dad yelled up the stairs. "The class starts in fifteen minutes!"

I'd have to just braid my hair in the car. I grabbed my camera and flew down the stairs and out the door.

"You ready for this?" he asked.

I shrugged. "Ready as I'll ever be!"

When I walked into the gym, I couldn't believe how huge it was. There were giant walls filled with brightly colored rocks and kids in harnesses everywhere. A loud pop song was blasting from the speakers, and a couple of girls were laughing and doing a popular TikTok dance to the music.

"All this was in the youth center the whole time?" I asked the camera, my eyes wide. Dad grinned.

"All right, teen beginners, over here!" A tall, college-aged guy with bright-blue hair held up a clipboard.

"That's us!" I told the camera. It was actually kind of exciting, like all of the Miacorns were there with me.

There was a small group of kids in the class, and Dad had to quickly ask their parents and the instructor permission to film, then went off to find the perfect angle. There were two other girls and two boys. One of the girls shot me a shy smile and told me she'd seen a few of my videos before.

"All right," Blue Hair said. "My name is Lee, and I'm the instructor for this class. Has anyone here been climbing before?"

The girl who said she'd seen my videos before raised her hand. "Um, but only once, a while ago."

"Great. Well, today, we'll be top climbing. That means using a rope and harness to stay safe, so you can't fall and get hurt. Safety is always first in my class, got it?"

We nodded. That made me feel a little better.

Everyone climbed into harnesses that Lee handed out, and he instructed me to take my long braid and tie it into a bun so that it didn't get caught in any of my equipment.

"Sorry I'm late! Is this the beginner class?" I turned to see another boy running up to join, and—

Oh...my goodness.

All of the heart-eye emojis.

The boy looked like he just fell out of a Netflix movie. He was tall and thin, with brown hair that barely flopped into his eyes, and deep tan skin. And his eyes—his *eyes!* They were *so* blue-green, like—

Mia! Focus! Not the time for crushing!

Especially because there was a camera pointed right at me. Not to mention my dad!

"Hi," he said, smiling at me.

"Hey. I'm Mia."

"Finn."

"Finn Torres?" Lee checked a box on his clipboard. "Great. Grab a harness."

He glanced up the rock-climbing wall. "Yikes, these are tall. Have you done this before?"

"No," I responded.

"So, what are you doing here? Sudden interest in climbing?" Finn asked with a grin.

I was just about to respond—although *how*, I wasn't sure, because it's not exactly easy to explain *Mia's Life* and the Miacorns when I'm *not* staring at a ridiculously cute boy—when Lee clapped his hands together.

"All right, gang. Everyone needs to put on a helmet. They may look dorky, but they're incredibly important. If something were to happen and you were to fall, it's essential that we protect those noggins." I wrinkled my nose at the heavy gray helmet he handed me.

"Helmet hair, anyone?" I muttered to the camera, holding up the helmet.

"Huh?" Finn asked.

"Nothing!" I squeaked.

"She's a vlogger," the quiet girl told Finn. "*Mia's Life*? This is for a video."

Finn's eyes went wide. "Woah—that's so cool! I was kinda wondering about the camera guy." I blushed about eighty-five shades of pink and heard Dad snicker from across the room. He was enjoying this way too much!

Kai walked us through chalking our hands and clipping our harnesses properly. I felt like I was wearing a gigantic diaper. Not exactly flirting-with-Finn material.

"All right," Lee said chipperly, "let's start with some basics. Your partner—and that's going to be *me* for today—is the belayer. When you're ready to climb, you say, 'On belay?' And if I'm ready, I respond, 'Belay on.' All together—say it for me."

"On belay," we started. "Belay on!"

"Then, when you're ready to climb, you say 'Climbing,' and I'll respond, 'Climb on.' That means we're good to go. If you don't hear your belayer respond, do *not* start climbing. That's the most important rule we have. We'll go over belaying in more advanced classes if that's something you're interested in, but for today, you're going to focus on climbing, and I'm going to support each of you. Who wants to tackle this beginner wall first and show us how it's done?"

One of the other boys volunteered to go first.

"Mia," Dad said, coming back toward me. "Let's snap some pics in your getup."

I posed with a thumbs-up and a cheesy grin in front of one of the walls. I actually forgot about Finn for half a second while I got a little excited. Maybe I could actually be good at this! It seemed pretty fun, and hey, I was connected to a rope the whole time. What was the worst that could happen?

"That boy's pretty cute, yeah?" Dad asked, smirking.

"*Dad!*" Couldn't he be a typical dad for once, horrified at his daughter dating?!

"Mia!" Lee called over. "Are you watching Sam? We're all learning from one another, here."

"Oops. Sorry." I hurried back over just in time to see Sam accidentally let go of a rock and go flying. Well, not exactly *flying*—he fell, like, six inches.

"Not to worry," called Lee. "That's why your belayer always has a hand on the rope!" He slowly lowered Sam to the ground. "Who's next?"

"I'll go," said Finn cheerfully. Now this I had to see. I noticed I wasn't the only girl looking either—the other two girls in our class were totally staring at him too!

After his "Climb on!" cue, Finn leaped up the wall with ease, and Lee walked us through how he was able to stretch and reach difficult rocks. Um, there was *no way* he was a beginner! I couldn't believe how good he was. He made it all the way to the top of the wall and reached out to ring the silver bell to signify he'd made it.

"That was terrific," said Lee, lowering Finn to the ground. "You should check out our intermediate class."

Finn blushed. OMG! He wasn't just athletic, he was humble. I could just picture it—we'd go on romantic rock-climbing dates together, just him and me. Together, we'd scale the highest walls, and our hands would touch while we reach out to rang the bell...

"Mia? Great!" said Lee. "Let's get you ready!"

"What?" I snapped back to life. Oops—my hand

had kind of floated in the air while I had kinda-sorta daydreamed about holding Finn's.

"All right, Mia!" Dad said encouragingly. "Let's do this thing."

I gulped. Lee connected the silver clasp to my harness and roped it through. I started to panic a little. How tight was this rope? What if it was frayed in places or something? What if I fell, or worse—completely humiliated myself in front of a million Miacorns? And *Finn?*

I tried to remember the time I'd gone skydiving. It was for a video I'd made last year. I'd been terrified to jump out of that airplane, but once I did it, it was completely exhilarating. Not just the rush of falling out of the plane, but of knowing I could do hard, scary things. I took a deep breath and put my foot on the first rock.

"*Mia.* Was I ready to belay you?"

"Oops. Sorry. On belay?"

"Belay on."

"Climbing," I said.

"Climb on!"

Okay. I could do this. I slowly moved my feet from one rock to another, reaching higher and higher. I could almost pretend Finn wasn't watching me. In fact, it was fun! I loved the feeling of pulling myself up, testing my own strength. I felt powerful, and it was something I'd never tried before. It was more about strength than coordination—I didn't have to catch a ball or do some complicated move. I just had to rely on my own body. I could do this! I *was* doing this!

I glanced down, which might have been a mistake. I was pretty high up. But Lee yelled up, "Great job! Keep going!" and Finn shouted, "Yeah, Mia!" That was all the encouragement I needed.

I hauled myself up on the next-highest rock, then glanced back down. I should give the Miacorns a wink—I wanted to do a peace sign or something, but I didn't trust myself to let go of the rocks for more than a half second without falling. But as I turned to look for my dad and the camera, something caught my eye, and—

Oh no—I was falling! And *fast!*

9

"I told you I'd humiliate myself," I grumbled to Dad. I hadn't fallen far; only six inches or so before Lee gently lowered me to the ground. But I *had* screamed—loudly. And whacked my knee on one of the rocks. Now it was throbbing. Not exactly my finest hour.

I glanced over and saw a class of little kids. They were climbing up the walls like experts! They were seriously incredible, and they looked even younger than Sienna. I wondered how much practice it would take to be that good. The truth was, I *had* enjoyed climbing—before my fall, of course. It had been different, but really fun. I actually wanted to try to climb again.

Dad chuckled. "Well, you're lucky you were being

safe. No harm, no foul. I saw you look around right before you fell. What distracted you?"

In the scariness of my fall, I'd almost forgotten why I'd screamed and let go. It was all because right there on the youth center bulletin board, there was a poster for space camp! Going to a real space camp would be the absolute perfect present for Sienna—no shipping required. It looked so cool, and I knew she'd have a blast. I needed to see what it was all about!

But I didn't want to tell Dad yet. I figured it would make a great surprise.

"Um...just got scared of being up so high, I guess," I said.

He opened his mouth to respond, but before he could, I felt a tap on my shoulder. I turned to see Finn, holding out a paper cup of water. I gesture wildly with my hands to get Dad to leave us alone.

"Here," he said. "That fall looked like it took your breath away."

Um, you're *what's taking my breath away,* I thought.

"Th-thanks." I took the water. "It wasn't that far."

He laughed. "No, but by the look on your face, it was plenty far enough."

I blushed.

"You looked great up there though." It was *his* turn to blush. "I mean...like, you looked like you knew what you were doing."

Was he *flirting* with me?! I wished Briony were here. I needed someone who spent most of her day surrounded by teenage boys! The truth was, I spent most of my time with my siblings and parents. I didn't exactly speak Cool Girl—more like, Klutzy Vlogger.

"You didn't tell me what *you're* doing here," I said. "You are definitely *not* a beginner. Why'd you sign up for the class? Just had a sudden urge to go rock climbing?"

"Um...it's kind of a long story."

"We have time," I said, nodding at the girl who was going next. She was creeping up the wall inch by inch while Lee coached her every move. She looked horrified, and she was barely a foot off the ground. "We may have all day, in fact."

He laughed. "Okay, okay! It's not that long, I guess. I teach here."

"In the gym?"

"No, but in the youth center. Upstairs. I teach art to elementary school kids."

Eyes of blue? Check. Heart of gold? Check.

"That's amazing!" I said. "I'm...I'm kind of into art too. I like to paint. Just for fun."

"Really? That's awesome," he said. "I teach on Saturday afternoons. Painting, mostly. I have such a great group of kids. It's my favorite part of the week. And we have a big art show Friday afternoon, where the kids get to hang their art on the walls and all of the parents and grandparents and stuff will come see what they've been doing. Some of the kids are so nervous to share their stuff, even though it's incredible!"

I nodded. "It can be hard to share what you create." My videos were one thing. But the thought of showing my own paintings was pretty scary. And even certain videos that revealed a lot sometimes felt intimidating to upload.

"Exactly! So, one of them... He's kind of this smart-aleck kid. But I like him. He says, 'Haven't you ever been afraid of anything?' And I was like, 'Of course. I'm actually afraid of heights—super afraid.' And he offers me a deal. That if I find a way to challenge myself with my fear of heights, he'll let me hang his painting at our art show."

My jaw dropped. "You're afraid of heights? But you were incredible up there!"

He grinned. "I was just thinking of my class. If they can overcome their fears, I can overcome mine, you know?"

I nodded. "Putting yourself out there."

"*Exactly.*"

Just like what I was doing with the fan takeovers. Getting out of my comfort zone. I wished I could find a way to tell Finn about them that didn't make me sound totally weird. But then, Lee clapped his hands together.

"All right, everyone. Our hour is up. If you had fun today, I hope you'll consider signing up for our intermediate class. It meets Monday evenings. And now that you know all of the safety rules, you can come to the gym at our open climbing times. You can see when those are on our website, and don't forget to use our hashtag if you share photos or videos from today!" He looked over at Dad, probably hoping we would advertise their classes in my video. I'd make sure to mention how well-prepared our instructor was, in case he saw it.

Everyone started to unhook their harnesses and got ready to leave. I flashed the camera a peace sign before reaching down to get out of my own gear. I felt so much freer without that giant thing hooked around my waist.

"Well," said Finn, "maybe I'll see you around at an open climb or something."

I gulped. "Yeah. Maybe. That would be... fun. Or something."

"Yeah," he grinned. "Or something."

He turned and left, that cute hair flopping as he walked away.

"Well, well, well," Dad said, smirking. "Our little Mia seems to have a big ol' crush."

"Stop," I hissed. I yanked off my helmet and handed it to Lee, hurrying away.

Dad made his way toward the exit.

"Hold on a second. I want to check out the bulletin

81

board and see if I can get any other video ideas." Really, I just wanted to get a closer look at that space camp poster.

Just like I thought, it looked perfect for Sienna! It was a weekend camp for kids who loved space. They'd get to go in a zero-gravity chamber, learn about what astronauts wore, and even eat that weird, prepackaged, freeze-dried space food Sienna had always wanted to try. She'd go absolutely nuts for it. The camp was for kids ages eight to eleven, and it was even in my price range.

I took out my phone and snapped a picture of the poster, putting it in my phone with a reminder set for that night to sign her up. It was so funny—in a way, the Miacorns *had* helped me find the gift, since they were the ones who had sent me rock climbing. I couldn't wait to tell them.

As we drove home from the gym, I flipped through the selfies I'd taken on my phone. It was pouring rain, and Dad was leaning forward just to see out the windshield.

It was like someone was spraying a hose right at our car.

"I can't believe I have to share a video where I scream, fall, and flail all over the place," I said.

"Wasn't that the point?" Dad said over the squeak of the windshield wipers working as fast as they would go.

"What do you mean?" I asked, wrinkling my nose at the thought of a million people laughing at me.

"Mia. You make these videos to share a piece of yourself with people. To connect with them. Not to show them what a great rock climber you are. You're *not* a great rock climber. You're a girl who tried something new, and did just okay at it, but had a lot of fun and made a new friend. You always say you don't like videos where girls are afraid to show themselves without makeup. Well, this is the same thing. You're kind of showing your *life* without makeup."

The more I thought about it, the more I realized Dad was making sense. My videos weren't just about me. They were about helping other people. Just like Finn wasn't really doing rock climbing for himself. He was doing it to inspire the kids in his class. To let them know that sometimes we have to do the things we're scared to do.

"You're right," I said.

Dad raised his eyebrows. "Should I record that? Keep it on file? Play it over and over again? Maybe it could be the new intro music for *Mia's Life*."

I laughed, just as a giant boom of thunder echoed across the night. "Stop. You know I love you, right?"

"I love you too, Mia," said Dad, turning the car into the driveway. "More than you know."

10

I spent hours going over all of the rock-climbing footage the day after meeting Finn at the class. Having Dad along had been perfect—he'd gotten a lot of great shots, from me talking about how nervous I was on the ride over to the moment I'd seen how big the walls were. It was going to make a terrific video. I even had to admit my fall was pretty funny. I barely fell, but I screamed as if I'd just seen a super gigantic spider. I knew when it got edited into slow motion and some sound effects were added, it would be hilarious.

I was trying to make a great video of the rock-climbing class, but not take too much time, since I still had to go back to the youth center to sign Sienna up for space camp. My plan was to print off a picture of the poster, or maybe grab a brochure and put it in a gigantic box. Her reaction to opening it was going to make such a fun video! I felt so relieved that I'd finally found the perfect gift. Sometimes Sienna got on my nerves—what little sister didn't?—but she was also one of my BFFs. I wanted to give her a birthday present she loved, one that made her feel like I knew her really well.

My muscles actually felt a little sore from climbing, which was nice. It had been different than my usual PE class, that was for sure! I was seriously considering going back and having another rock-climbing adventure. Who knew that I would enjoy climbing up a fake wall so much?

I put the camera just on me, with my hair in long braids. Sometimes after I filmed a video, I'd do a clip where I explained what doing the challenge felt like. I often had to use my ring light to get the coloring of the video just right, but with the natural morning light streaming in through my window, it was perfect. Sienna was at a tutoring session, Dad and Mom had taken the little kids for a walk, and it was just me and my thoughts. They kept returning to the memory of Finn, and how great it had been talking to him at the gym.

"Rock climbing wasn't something that came naturally to me," I told the Miacorns. "In fact, it made me incredibly nervous. I didn't know if I was going to fall, or get hurt, or just embarrass myself. But I decided to go for it, and you know what? I had fun. I liked trying something new, and I liked learning a new skill. And..." I paused. Should I share about Finn? Why not? That was part of my real life, right? And I was all about keeping it real. "I made a new friend. Well, at least...I hope we become friends. He was so cute, you guys. And get this— he actually works at the youth center teaching art to kids. I mean, how adorable is that?! He was really sweet, and when I fell—*ugh*—he brought me water, and we started talking and just kind of clicked. I hope I see him again next time I go to the youth center. *If* I go to the youth center." I bit my lip. "Usually, I like to think of myself as a pretty confident person, but these fan takeovers have showed me how much I need to be brave in my real life like I am brave with you all. Like, I can talk about my period on YouTube, but I got nervous talking to a boy? That doesn't feel right. So... Thank you, Miacorns. Thanks for reminding me to take chances and be brave in my everyday life."

I reached over and clicked off the camera.

For a quick second, I got nervous. What if Finn saw the video? *No*, I assured myself—there was no way he was going to leave the class and look up *Mia's Life*. I was checking him out, but surely he wasn't as interested in getting to know me.

Was he?

11

"Is that a carrot?"

Briony looked up at me, then back at her painting on the backdrop. "It's supposed to be a rocket ship."

"Why is it orange?"

"I don't know!" Briony threw her hands in the air. "Is there a rule saying rockets can't be orange?"

I squinted at it. "But...what's the green stuff up on top?"

"It was supposed to be smoke..."

I put my hand on her shoulder. "Briony. Put down the paintbrush before someone gets hurt."

She laughed. "Okay, okay! I'm not exactly an artist. But I *can* make a mean space-themed playlist to blast out in your backyard. Can that be my new job?"

"Deal," I said with a giggle.

Briony had come over to help me and Mom make decorations for Sienna's party. The two of us were in our grubbiest clothes, attempting to paint a backdrop, while Mom blew up a thousand balloons and almost passed out. Dad had taken Karma, Koa, and Sienna to the park and out for some dessert.

"I can't wait to see her face when she walks into the backyard," I said excitedly. "She's going to totally freak out!"

"*I* can't wait to see her face when she opens up your present," Briony responded.

"Agreed," said Mom. "That was such a great idea, Mia."

"I have to go back tomorrow and actually sign her up, though," I said. "Don't let me forget! I was going to go today but time totally got away from me with these decorations and answering all of my Instagram comments. People *loved* the rock-climbing video!"

Briony reached over and dotted my knee with hot pink paint. "Um, that's not *all* they loved."

"Mia and Finn, sitting in a tree..." Mom sang.

I could feel my face getting hot. "You two are such dorks. Nobody sings that song anymore, Mom."

"Someone's *grumpy*," sang Briony.

I laughed. "I'm sorry! I just... It feels kind of weird, letting all of the Miacorns in on my crush. But I *do* have a crush, and I tell them everything! I don't know what to do. I'm probably never going to see him again, anyway."

It was true—I let my fans into so many aspects of my life. I wasn't afraid to talk about puberty or which bra I bought first. I didn't mind talking about acne or showing them my face without makeup. I loved telling them what I was really going through and really thinking. Wasn't this just another part of my life? Was I hiding something if I didn't tell them about it?

"Wait," said Briony, standing up from our massive

canvas to stretch. "Didn't you say he works at the youth center?"

"Yeah? So?"

"*So*," she said with a wicked grin, "don't you have to go back there to sign Sienna up for space camp?"

I froze. "Oh no. I didn't think about that. What if I see him?"

Mom furrowed her brow. "It's the twenty-first century. You're telling me they don't have online sign-ups?"

"It's a community youth center, not NASA," I grumbled.

Briony squealed, clapping her hands together. "This is so perfect! You'll go sign her up. You'll casually glance across the room. And there he'll be, like, standing there with his cute hair flopping in the wind..."

"We'll be indoors. Not sure how windy it's going to be," I commented.

"You'll lock eyes," Briony continued dramatically,

"and then—the moment—he walks over! He grabs your hand! He—"

"Probably doesn't even remember my name," I said.

Mom laughed. "You girls are too much."

Briony grabbed my phone with what could only be described as a mischievous smile.

"Um...what are you doing?"

She quickly typed a few things, then turned to show me and Mom. There was a photo of me from rock climbing—I looked pretty cute, if I do say so myself! And there was another Instagram poll drafted on the screen.

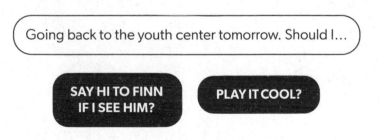

"Post it!" Mom cheered.

"Oh my gosh," I groaned, burying my face in my hands. "I don't know..."

Briony held her finger dangerously over the Post button. "Tell me the Miacorns wouldn't totally love it."

"Of course they would," I said. "Ugh...fine! Hit Post!" She did, and the three of us screamed like Sienna and her friends.

"If they do vote for saying hi to Finn...I don't know what I would say after I said hi. I would probably just hide. Because I'm awkward and klutzy and not at all sophisticated, remember?"

"Uh-uh," Briony said firmly, grabbing my shoulders. "Not going to let you talk down on yourself like that. Awkward? A little. Klutzy? One hundred percent. But you are Mia Fizz! You are a business owner! You are a YouTube sensation! You are *not afraid* to talk to cute boys!"

Everyone should have a BFF like Briony. I could feel her words coursing through my veins. She was right, wasn't she? I was Mia Fizz! I could do this!

And that's when I took a step to hug her, stepped on a roll of tape, and fell backward—hard—landing on my butt.

I looked up at her and Mom, who were both frozen.

"But I am, apparently, unable to take three steps without falling," I said. They laughed so hard I didn't know if they'd ever catch their breaths. When was I ever going to stop being so uncoordinated?

Dad finally returned with my three siblings in tow, and Briony stayed for bedtime, reading Karma a story while Dad put Koa down and Mom tucked Sienna in. I checked on our canvas for the photo booth—dry and perfect, even if Briony's rocket did still look like something a bunny would munch on.

While I listened to all of the bedtime-routine chaos going down, I wondered what this time of night was like in Finn's house. Did he have siblings? Were his parents married? Did he live in a house or an apartment or an RV? I really knew hardly nothing about him. I wished I could sit down with him and learn all about his life— where he came from, what he liked to do...

Maybe I *could* talk to him again. I hadn't stopped thinking about him.

I pulled out my phone to check the Instagram poll. OMG! Only twenty percent of people had suggested I play it cool, meaning eighty percent of people wanted me to go say hi to Finn!

Um, what the heck was I supposed to say to Finn? What was I supposed to wear? Should I film it? Or would that be too weird? But if I didn't, would the Miacorns be upset?

I felt like I was going to throw up. I flopped down onto the couch and clicked on who had voted yes, scrolling through the thousands of names. Sienna—shocker. Mom too—traitor!

And then—

Wait.

No. It couldn't be! This was beyond an OMG situation. This was put-me-on-Briony's-orange-rocket-and-blast-me-to-the-moon situation.

Because, right there, was a photo of a smiling, happy *Finn.*

Finn had found my Instagram and seen the poll!

12

"I don't think it's the *total* end of the world though."

Briony and I were sipping mugs of hot chocolate made with almond milk and snacking on dry cereal while Mom and Dad washed the dishes. Sienna, Karma, and Koa were all tucked into bed, but I refused to let Briony leave. She was the one who'd gotten me into this mess!

My room felt incredibly cozy. It was dark outside, but we'd lit a few candles and turned on a dim lamp instead of the harsh overhead light, and I felt like we were in our own safe little bubble. Too bad we were discussing the most mortifying thing that had ever happened to me.

"That's where you're wrong!" I said as Mom and Dad

walked in. "It is completely and utterly the end of the world."

"Mia," Dad laughed, "I was there too, remember? I saw the two of you talking. He seemed like he had a bit of a crush on you too! And he looked up your social media handle after the class. He wouldn't have done that if he didn't think you were interesting. He would have just forgotten he'd ever met you. He *didn't*, though, did he?"

As soon as I had realized it was Finn on my poll, I had tried to check out his Instagram profile, but he kept it pretty locked down. All I could see was his profile picture—him in a blue jacket, grinning at the camera. He was even cuter than I remembered! How was that possible? But it was strange that he now knew so much about me, and I still knew next to nothing about him.

I buried my face in my hands. "This means he's definitely seen the video, right? The one where I talk about how cute he was? Why didn't I think about this?!"

Briony rubbed my back sympathetically. "You're forgetting an extremely important part of this equation."

"What?"

"That he voted yes! Obviously, he likes you too. He wants you to come say hi. Don't miss out on a really great opportunity just because you're embarrassed, Mia."

"He likes me *now*," I explained. "But what if he goes back and watches all of my old videos? The ones where I'm talking about getting *boobs*? He's going to see a video about *boobs*!"

Briony shrugged. "So what? They're just a body part."

But I just kept thinking of new videos I'd never want a guy I had a crush on to see. Videos where I asked my parents embarrassing questions, videos where I cried, videos where I tried on new bikinis...

"You're not embarrassed of *Mia's Life*, are you?" Dad asked.

"No. Of course not. I love doing *Mia's Life*." And it was true. Making videos was my passion, and so was

101

connecting with my viewers. I didn't have anything to apologize for.

But at the same time, *Mia's Life* was so open. I shared a ton with my viewers, and I was starting to wonder if it was too much. Because *Mia's Life* wasn't my life—it was a *part* of my life. A part I absolutely loved, but still, just a part.

Maybe too big of one.

"I'm just feeling weird," I said. "I didn't think he was

going to find my channel. And now I feel kind of...naked. That's all."

Mom nodded sympathetically. "This kind of stuff can be so hard. I remember these days very well." Mom had me when she was only sixteen. Things had been really hard for her, but at the same time, the fact that we were so close in age made us feel, well, close. Closer than your average mother and daughter. And when she said she remembered things, I knew she really did.

"Wait a second," I said, getting an idea.

"I don't like that look," said Briony, pointing her mug at me. "That's your I-have-a-brilliant-plan look."

"I *do* have a brilliant plan!" I squealed. I whipped out my phone and opened up the poll. "*Look!*"

She looked. "Yep, ninety-two percent of people want you to say hi to Finn. Isn't that what we're talking about?"

"It's up to ninety-two percent? Oh my gosh—no! Don't distract me. The *poll*. Read what it says."

Mom leaned over Briony's shoulder and squinted at

the phone. "It's asking if people want you to say hi to Finn if you see him, or if you should play it cool."

I grinned triumphantly. "See?"

Everyone stared at me.

"*If* I see him," I said. "*If* I see him! But maybe...I won't! So, Briony, maybe if *you* went to go sign Sienna up instead..."

"No way," she said flatly.

"Come on," I whined. "You owe me. Remember the time in first grade when Nico Fitzgerald called you a baby for not wanting to jump off the swings, and I poured my orange juice on him?"

"Remember the fifty million times since then I've filmed you doing stuff like wearing bright-blue rhinestone makeup to the mall?" she countered.

"Fair."

"Besides," said Briony, "I can't sign her up. They're going to ask all of these questions I won't have answers to, like her birthday."

"Um, hello? Her birthday's on Saturday."

"Oh, yeah," giggled Briony.

Dad sat down on the bed next to me and shook his head. "I don't think that's fair, Mia. Your viewers want *you* to go. They want to see you explore your crush. That's the whole point!"

"But maybe I don't want to show them," I argued.

"You don't have to actually film it," Mom said. "You just have to actually follow through. Then you could tell the story afterward for the Miacorns without actually showing them. Besides, you shouldn't be filming much in the youth center where there are lots of kids around without getting their parents' permission first anyway." She had a point. "Come on. What's the worst that could happen?"

"I could fall on my face and make a total fool of myself?"

"Didn't you already do that at rock-climbing class?" Briony pointed out. "You did make a fool of yourself, and guess what—he liked you anyway. Don't forget that he voted yes too!"

"Maybe I could get Sienna something else for her birthday," I said. "That way, I'll just never have to go to the youth center again."

"Ever again?" Mom asked skeptically. "Not sure how realistic that is, Mia."

"Besides, I thought you couldn't think of anything else," said Briony.

"I'm full of ideas!" I insisted. "I could get her…a cat."

"No," Mom said immediately.

"A…Wonder Woman poster?"

"She has two," Dad responded.

"New animal ears," I said proudly. That was brilliant—Sienna loved wearing cat-ear headbands.

"That's what I got her," Briony admitted.

I moaned, dropping my face into my hands. "Isn't being my little sister a present enough?"

"Mia Fizz," Mom scolded me.

I rolled my eyes. "Fine. I'll do it. I'll go to the youth center, I'll sign up her up for space camp, and it'll be the best present she's ever gotten. But you have to come with me." I pointed at my best friend. "You got me into this mess, and you're going to help me get out."

We clinked our mugs together.

"Deal!" cheered Briony.

13

"This isn't exactly what your viewers had in mind," said Briony.

It was the next afternoon—the day before Sienna's party. I was out of time. If I wanted to be able to gift her space camp for her ninth birthday, I had to make the trip to the youth center. *Today.*

But something had occurred to me that morning while Briony was at school and I was attempting to read *Jane Eyre.*

I had to go to the youth center.

But...did Mia Fizz?

"It's perfect," I said confidently, looking at my disguise in the mirror. I had tucked my long blond hair up under a bright-red wig and had on some clunky, square glasses with purple frames and no lenses. Thank goodness we kept all of our old Halloween costumes.

"It's...something," said Briony.

"Now, I just need an outfit that doesn't feel like me."

"But I don't get it." Briony flopped down onto my bed. "Don't you *want* to say hi to him and get to know him?"

"Yes," I admitted. "But...not on a dare from Instagram, okay?"

"The Miacorns wanted you to talk to him!"

"*If* I saw him," I reminded her. "And with this disguise, even if *he* saw *me*, he wouldn't know it! This is the perfect solution. And it will still make a funny video—I'll tell the Miacorns all about it."

Briony and I went into my parents' room and I opened up my dad's closet. "There will totally be *something* I can wear in here. Dad has some weird stuff." I started flipping through his clothes.

"Your parents don't really have that much stuff," Briony commented, looking around their room.

"We travel a lot," I reminded her, "and they don't like having to lug a ton of clothes around."

"I guess that makes sense. Hey, what about that trench coat?"

"I would never wear a trench coat!"

"That's my point," said Briony, pulling it down. "Honestly, would your *dad* ever wear a trench coat?"

"It's vegan!" I said, checking out the tag. "Whew. Fake suede. I don't think I could do the real thing."

"I know, but...a trench coat? I'm just saying. I could never see your dad wearing this!"

"Maybe it's vintage, or from another Halloween costume or something. Whatever." I pulled it on. "It fits! Sort of. How does it look!"

Briony laughed. "Very *not* Mia Fizz, that's for sure. What about pants?"

"I've got an idea," I said, digging through my mom's

dresser. "She has these maternity leggings that are so..."
I found them and pulled them out. "Out there!"

Briony giggled. "Zebra stripes? Really?"

"They're from a million years ago. I think she just keeps them because they're really comfortable." I wiggled into the pants, then checked myself out in my parents' giant mirror. My look was ridiculous— ridiculously amazing!

"I look nothing like myself," I said proudly. "Finn won't even recognize me."

Briony wrinkled her nose. "It's weird. I mean, he'll see the video where you explain that you went in disguise. It's kind of like you're digitally flirting without interacting."

"I know," I said. I took a selfie in my mirror, sticking my tongue out at my goofy look. But I just saved it—I couldn't post it until after we were safely back at home! I wondered if I should make an alter ego out of my costume, like Miranda Sings. I watched a ton of YouTubers myself, to get ideas for new videos and explore other people's lives. One of my favorites was the Rybka Twins—I wondered if Briony would ever dress in a matching outfit with me, and we could try and convince people *we* were twins. That would make a fun video...

"On the plus side," said Briony, bringing me back to Earth, "you've definitely gotten a kick of creativity back in your videos. Your views are way up, and people are totally loving the lifestyle, fan-takeover-type videos. Not that they *didn't* love the makeup ones. But it seems like they're having fun watching something new!" That was good to hear. I wanted to make content the Miacorns enjoyed. Besides, I could always go back to making makeup videos if I felt like it.

"I'm having fun making something new too," I admitted. "Even if it is making me nervous. This is reminding me of how we loved to play dress-up when we were kids."

"It's reminding *me* of getting ready for dances and stuff with girls from school," said Briony.

"Does Shanti still always make you listen to eighties rock-and-roll while everyone does their hair?" I asked with a giggle.

Briony rolled her eyes. "Oh my gosh, *yes*. I needed you and your playlists to save us before the back-to-school bash!"

"I haven't seen those girls in forever. Maybe I should have everyone over or something," I mused.

"Yeah, maybe," said Briony.

It wasn't often that I missed going to a regular school. Homeschooling was a great fit for me and my family. I loved that I wasn't stuck behind a desk! But sometimes, I wondered if I was missing out on stuff like school dances. Briony didn't seem to think they were that much fun, but her pictures always made it look like she was having a blast. Besides, if I went to a regular school, maybe I wouldn't be so awkward around boys. After all, Briony and Shanti sat next to boys all day, in math and history and Spanish. Shanti was practically a professional flirter, and I was still very much in the minor leagues.

But maybe today was my first time at bat. Digital flirting—I could make it a thing!

"Okay, let's see if this works," I said, handing my camera to Briony. "Can you film me?"

Together, we left my parents' room and walked down to the kitchen, where Mom and Dad were getting some work done on their laptops while Karma and Koa munched on some watermelon. Sienna was over at a friend's house, because we were going to get the backyard ready for her party as soon as Briony and I got back from the youth center. I slowly crept down the hall, with Briony quietly following me. We reached the kitchen and stood in front of the table, waiting patiently for someone to look up. When Dad finally did—

He screamed like a little kid who'd just seen a monster in his closet!

Which, of course, made Mom scream.

Which, *of course*, made the little kids cry.

Suddenly, the entire house was loud and chaotic as Dad laughed hysterically at my outfit while Mom tried to calm down Karma and Koa.

"What on earth, Mia?" Mom asked. "Are those my maternity leggings?"

"What do you think?" I asked, giving a twirl. "Will Finn recognize me?"

"Not in a million years," said Dad. "But isn't that defeating the point?"

"The point is to make a video people enjoy watching. This will totally do that!" I said confidently.

"I'm not talking about the point of *Mia's Life*," Dad said. "I'm talking about the point of you getting to talk to the boy you have a crush on!"

"I told her all of this, for the record," said Briony.

"Come on," I said, throwing my fake-suede-covered arm around Briony. "We have a cute boy to strategically avoid!"

14

My uncle loves the movie *Rocky*. I'd always thought it was pretty dorky how he gets to the top of the steps and pumps his fist in the air. But that's the exact theme music I had in my head as I walked toward the youth center, disguise and all.

"We look ridiculous," Briony giggled. "Remember when you were Goldilocks for Halloween? This is ten times weirder!"

I couldn't help but laugh too. Soon, we were laughing so hard that people who biked by us on the sidewalks were giving us weird looks. I couldn't help it—this was one of the many reasons why Briony was my best friend!

She was so funny and always willing to help me out in sticky situations.

Like Operation Sign Sienna Up for Camp While Avoiding Finn.

When we got to the youth center, it looked packed. And that's when I saw it—the signs advertising the youth center art show!

How could I have forgotten?

The art show for the kids Finn taught.

The art show was *tonight*!

"Briony!" I squealed. "We need to go home."

"Why?"

"I forgot something!"

"What did you forget."

"My...my lucky pen," I said as I turned around rapidly. "My lucky pen that I take everywhere with me. No time to explain. Let's go home!"

Briony grabbed my elbow, yanking me back. "Not so fast. They'll have pens at the front desk for you to use—I'm sure of it. You don't need this mysterious lucky pen I've never heard of."

"Right," I said, smacking my forehead with my palm. "What I meant was that I'm...not feeling well."

"Oh, no! Did you eat something? Or is it a headache?" Briony looked *nervous*. Like she was actually worried about me being sick. I didn't want to freak her out, but I did want to get the heck out of there!

"Um...not exactly. I guess I meant I'm more, you know, heartsick." I nodded toward the art show sign.

Briony glanced at it, and I could see the wheels turning in her mind as she put two and two together. "*Finn's* art show! So he *is* here!"

I nodded miserably. "He's here, and when he sees me, it's going to be totally embarrassing. He heard me call him cute in front of a million people!"

Briony laughed. "Hello? I thought we'd been over this. Isn't that the whole point of the disguise?"

"I guess," I groaned. "But to be honest, I just thought

the disguise was fun. I didn't think we would actually see him here!"

"Well, maybe we won't," Briony pointed out. "I mean, look how crowded this place is! Maybe it actually ups your chances of going unnoticed. He could be busy helping set up or direct people around."

I gulped. "Let's hope so."

"Come on." Briony dragged me toward the entrance. As we walked up the perfectly landscaped walkway, I tried to keep one thing in my mind: Sienna. My sister deserved an incredible birthday present, no matter how nervous I was! I kept trying to picture her face when she learned she was going to space camp. It was worth any potential embarrassment.

"Okay," said Briony, "ready for this?"

We stood a few feet in front of the door, watching as people streamed in and out. Tons of people were checking out the art show. I loved seeing the parents walk in with giant cameras—they were so proud of their kids! I bet Finn was really proud too. I wondered if the kid who had been nervous ended up displaying his art after Finn had gone climbing. I hoped so. I wished I could go to the show myself and see whatever Finn had created. It was sure to be amazing.

"Ready," I said. "But first, maybe we should check to see if the coast is clear."

Briony nodded. "Like, peek in the window? Check out the main area first?"

"Exactly." But just as I leaned in to peer through the window, someone pushed the door open!

Oof! I went flying; I waspushedbackward, then tripped over my shoes. I tumbled to

the ground and rolled down the two steps in front of the door, shrieking the whole time. Suddenly, I was laying in the grass, covered in dirt, and my wig and glasses were nowhere to be seen. I almost wished someone had caught it on camera.

"Um...Mia? Hey."

It was Finn!

15

"What are you doing here?"

My heart was racing, and my face turned hot. I couldn't believe it—there was Finn, standing right in front of me! Instead of wearing a harness and a helmet, he had on a worn green T-shirt and blue jeans. He even had a fleck of paint on his shoulder.

Well, Finn, here's the thing. I took a poll among the Miacorns and they all wanted me to talk to you if I saw you. But I'm a big chicken, so I thought if I wore a disguise, you definitely wouldn't recognize me, and I'd never have to see your face again, even though I think you're totally cute and I really want to get to know you better. So I stole a bunch of stuff from my parents to make a fake disguise, dragged my bestie here, and am working hard to avoid, well, YOU.

"Oh, you know," I said, holding a hand in front of my eyes to block the sun. "Just...hanging around..."

He reached his hand down. Oh my gosh—he wanted to help me up! I glanced at Briony, who gave me an excited thumbs-up. I took his hand and he slowly tugged me to my feet.

"Are you okay?" he asked. "I'm so sorry. There's so many people coming in and out of the doors—I should have checked to see if someone was there."

"No! It was my fault. Don't worry about it. I'm just a little...klutzy. As you saw at climbing class," I reminded him. I was doing this! I was talking to Finn!

He laughed. "Hey, now! Don't sell yourself short. I thought you did great. Did you come back to climb some more? Or were you going to check out the art show?"

"Now that I'm here, I'd love to see some of the art," I told him. "I'll check it out. But I actually came to sign my sister up for the space camp. It's happening in a couple of weeks, and it looks really fun. They're going to do a zero-gravity thing and learn all about the solar system, plus they get to wear astronaut suits and eat freeze-dried food. She absolutely loves anything to do with outer space, and it's her birthday tomorrow!"

"Oh, wow! She'll love that," he said. "Sienna, right?"

"How did you—" I froze, feeling my cheeks flush again. How did he know? Because of *Mia's Life*, obviously!

It was his turn to look a little embarrassed. "Okay, okay! I confess. After we met and I heard you were a YouTuber, I went and looked up your videos. They were so funny and sweet and just...really, really fun to watch. Your family seems really tight."

"We are," I said.

"There was just something really cool about that, you know? Anyway, I may have been up half the night binge-watching. Me and every teenage girl in the world, apparently!" We laughed.

"So, listen," he said. "What you asked about Rock-Climbing Boy?"

Oh my gosh! I hoped Briony was hearing every single word!

"Yeah?" I asked. What was he about to say? *That was totally weird? I never want you to mention me again? Stay away from me, YouTuber?*

"Um...I think you should talk to him. If you see him." And then, he winked. He *winked*! My first-ever wink from a real live cute boy standing right in front of me!

I giggled nervously, probably sounding totally ridiculous. "Um, okay. I will. If I see him."

He laughed. "You might see him at the youth center's big fundraiser, a week from Saturday. Just...so you know."

Was he *asking me out*?

"Okay," I said, smiling. "Well, if I see him there, I'll definitely talk to him."

He grinned. "I should get back in there. Later."

"Later."

He turned to go back into the youth center, but just as he was about to open the door, he glanced over his shoulder.

"Oh, and Mia? No disguise required next time."

He disappeared into the center, and my heart fell fifteen stories into my stomach.

"Oh. My. Gosh!" Briony shrieked in my ear. "Mia! That was the most adorable meet-cute ever! They will be making Netflix movies about this exact moment! Do you realize that?!"

I grabbed her shoulders. "He kind of asked me out, right?"

"He *totally* asked you out!" she squealed. We jumped up and down like a couple of...well, a couple of best friends. Which was exactly what we were.

"Come on," she said. "We need to go sign Sienna up for camp. Or did you forget the entire reason we were here?"

"I'm sorry, did you *see* those eyes? Can you blame me?" I teased.

"Don't go getting all mushy-gushy on me."

"Hey, maybe he has a friend."

"Maybe," Briony giggled. "But I should tell you... There's a boy at school I've been talking to."

"What?! Briony Baker! Way to hold back extremely important information!" We went into the youth center, feeling the air-conditioning blasting us in our faces, and meandered our way to the information desk.

"I just felt like we needed to focus on Finn, and mixing things up for the Miacorns, and Sienna's birthday," Briony explained. "There's always so much going on in the life of Mia Fizz, you know? I didn't want to steal any of your spotlight."

That made me feel terrible. "Listen," I told her. "It doesn't matter if every single day I fall from a new rock-climbing wall and meet a new soul mate. You're my best friend, and I care if you're crushing on a guy. Nothing will ever come between us or be more important than that! Okay?"

"Okay, okay!"

"And when we walk home, you are spilling *all* the details," I informed her. "It's your solemn best friend duty."

"Deal." She smiled. I made a mental note: I'd spent a lot of time with Briony this week, but I needed to spend more time going forward asking her about *her* life. Just because she didn't vlog it to a million people didn't mean that it wasn't important!

I stepped up to the desk. "I need to register someone for the space camp at the end of the month, please."

A tall woman with long braids smiled at me. "Sure thing. Here's a form. If they're under eighteen years old, they'll also need to bring along this signed permission slip on the first day."

I grabbed the form she handed me and took the brochure she passed over as well. There were all the space camp details, and on the cover was a girl who looked almost like Sienna. She was rocking a full-on astronaut suit and smiling super wide, throwing a peace sign in the air. Soon, that would be Sienna.

"You did it," giggled Briony. "You found the perfect present."

I snapped a quick selfie with the brochure to share with the Miacorns—after Sienna's party, of course. I couldn't wait to see her face when she opened her gift!

16

That night, I couldn't sleep. I tossed and turned in bed, running through the itinerary for Sienna's party, reliving my moment with Finn, and remembering what Briony had said. I was Mia Fizz—a small business owner and a YouTube sensation, and I wasn't afraid to talk to cute boys. But I was also just awkward, klutzy Mia, who was sometimes shy and didn't feel comfortable sharing every little thing about my life.

I knew what I had to do.

I got out of bed as quietly as I could so that I didn't wake up the rest of my family—after all, we had a big day tomorrow, with Sienna's birthday. I turned on my ring light and then my camera. I was completely barefaced, in just my pajama shirt. I looked like *I* was the one turning nine tomorrow! But I didn't care—I had something I needed to share.

"Hey Miacorns. Welcome back to *Mia's Life*," I told the camera. It sat there blinking at me.

"So, you'll all be pleased to know that I *did* end up meeting Finn again, although I didn't look my absolute best..." I paused so a photo of me in my disguise could be edited in. "But I ran into him—literally. As in, I may or may not have a bruise on my elbow from the encounter."

It would have been so perfect to have footage of that fall! Oh, well. I took a deep breath. Time to get real.

"And...I'm going back to rock climbing. I really, really enjoyed it, even though I'm not exactly a professional yet. It made me feel confident and strong, and those are feelings I'm always trying to embrace! That being said, I don't think I'm going to make any more videos about Finn. The truth is, I want to share everything with the Miacorns! And I do—ninety-nine percent of the time.

But I need to keep some things a little more personal, between me and my bestie and my family."

I bit my lip. I hoped nobody was going to be mad at me. Sometimes, fans wanted to know every single thing about my life. Most of the time, I loved inviting them in. But not everything was made for the eyes of the internet, and I knew that. Mom and Dad were always telling me that if I didn't want to make a video about something, I didn't have to. I could talk about acne or boobs or getting my period. I could show myself falling ridiculously or explain a fight I had with Sienna. But this thing with Finn—whatever it was—just wasn't something I felt comfortable sharing.

"I hope you guys understand," I said. "I love the Miacorns. In some ways, we're all like one big family. But this is something that doesn't belong in my videos anymore. But I know you're all super excited for Sienna's birthday party tomorrow, and I love that through the show, I can bring you all with me. Party for a million, anyone?" I giggled. "Anyway, thank you for supporting me. Thanks for encouraging me to step out of my comfort zone too—we'll have a lot more fan takeovers in the future, because they've been a total blast. And most importantly, thanks for letting me be me. Not just Mia Fizz, YouTuber, but Mia Fizz, real live girl."

I reached over and turned the camera off. I had one last thing to do. After this week's experiment, I felt myself getting braver. I had unlocked some super well of confidence I didn't even know that I'd had. First, I clicked over to Instagram and requested to follow Finn. Then I shot him a message.

> Tomorrow's my sister's birthday party, if you want to see her get pumped for space camp in person! If you send me your number, I can text you deets.

What's the worst thing he could say—no? Then, fine. I'd live. And hey, he *might* say yes. Life was all about taking chances, wasn't it?

Now, I could finally fall asleep, with a smile on my face.

17

"Happy birthday, dear Sienna! Happy birthday to you!"

The entire backyard burst into cheers, and Sienna blew out her nine pink candles Mom had stuck in a large, moon-shaped cake. Her party was a raging success!

Sienna's birthday morning had started off great. I'd gotten up early to help Dad make her vegan pancakes with fruit and coconut yogurt before she got up, and when she came into the kitchen, we sang her the first round of "Happy Birthday" while filming her reaction. She loved it! Then, we showed her the backyard, which took everything to the next level. She had simply walked around, wide-eyed, taking it all in.

Mom and Dad had done an amazing job of making

the backyard look like outer space—well, as much as a yard *can* look like outer space. There was the photo backdrop Briony and I had painted, carrot rocket ship and all. The buffet table was amazing, with star-shaped pizzas, mini sparkling popcorn ball comets, the beautiful cake pops, and more. Mom had finally gotten the balloon arch figured out, and there were signs everywhere shaped like little suns reminding everyone to use the hashtag #SiennaTurnsNine. But the best part of all was the projector in front of the fence, making shooting stars dance and squirm their way across the yard. It was perfect. Every time I glanced at my little sister, she had a huge smile on her face. Koa and Karma were wandering around, too, their faces already smeared with cake pop as they danced in front of the lights. The weather had cooperated too, and it was a beautiful day.

I'd spent most of the morning filming the party being set up. My parents had worked so hard getting everything just right. When guests arrived, I was able to film that too;

I had a vision of doing a time lapse, so people could see how quickly the yard had filled! All of Sienna's classmates were there, and they looked like they were having a great time. Briony's curated Space Tunes playlist was rocking as well—we were currently listening to "Rocket Man." She was trying to wipe Karma's face off, and the two-year-old was stubbornly running away every chance she got.

But now, I'd handed the camera off to Dad so that I could enjoy myself hands-free for a bit. He was going to help me get some footage that could be edited together, making Sienna's party its very own video. Sienna was thrilled—she loved being featured on my channel! She looked great, too, in a shimmery silver dress with a bright blue bow in her hair. Mom had taken what felt like a hundred pictures of her that morning.

"Happy birthday, sister," I said, throwing my arms around her.

"Thanks, Mia!" she said. "I can't wait to open your present."

"It's pretty...out of this world," I said happily.

Just then, her jaw dropped. I turned to see what she was looking at.

"Mia!" There was Finn, walking into our yard.

"Wait! Isn't that—" I clapped my hand over Sienna's mouth as quickly as I could.

"Finn! Oh my gosh...um, hi!" I said.

He grinned. "You didn't think I'd come?"

"Well, I hoped you would," I admitted, blushing a little. When I'd woken up and seen that he'd responded to my message, I had quickly texted him our address and the time the party was starting. But the fact that he had actually come felt incredible! Taking a chance had totally paid off.

I shot my dad a glance, and he quickly turned the camera on Mom, who was giving a tour of the party. He understood what I had been saying about Finn—that this was something I wanted to keep off-camera from here on out. I loved that Mom and Dad were supportive of me filming *and* supportive of me not filming. I knew I was lucky to have them.

"I'm glad you're here," I said. "How did the art show go?"

"It was amazing," he replied. "I loved seeing the kids really bust out of their comfort zones, you know? And, hey... I think my rock climbing may have even inspired them. I liked it too—the climbing. I'm thinking of going back to the intermediate class."

"Me too!" I told him. "Well, I think I might need to repeat the beginner unit. But I had so much fun."

"Maybe we can go climbing together sometime," he said. "If you wanted?"

"Yeah," I said, blushing. "That would be really f—"

"Oh, my gosh! Mia! Is that Finn from your channel?!" One of my sister's friends leaped in between us. "This is, like, so cool! The famous Finn!"

Finn smiled at her, but he looked like he felt a little uncomfortable. "Um...yeah. Hi. I'm Finn."

"Brianna," she said, flipping her hair over her shoulder. "And I—"

"Was just going to check out the snacks," Sienna interrupted, yanking her friend away. *Sorry*, she mouthed to me.

"That was...more than awkward," I told Finn.

He laughed. "Yeah, well. Your channel is your life. I get that."

"Not my *whole* life," I reminded him. "But hey—that was nice of Sienna."

"She seems like a pretty cool kid."

"She is."

"All right, everyone!" Mom shouted, gesturing toward the gift table. "The birthday girl is about to open her presents!"

I raised an eyebrow at Finn. "You coming? I heard a rumor that YouTuber Mia Fizz absolutely slayed the present game this year."

He grinned. "Wouldn't miss it for the world."

18

Dad was all set up with the camera, so that you could see Sienna open gift after gift. She was excitedly tearing the wrapping paper off books, clothes, and board games.

"Wow—the Shimmer Sparkle Lab! This is where you can make your own lip balm. I've wanted this for *ages*. Thanks, Brianna!" Sienna squealed.

Brianna smiled. "No problem. It was on your wish list, after all."

I turned to Briony and Finn as I muttered, "All that stress, and it turns out she had a wish list I could have looked at?" They both snickered.

"Okay," Mom said excitedly. "It looks like there's just

one gift left." She held out a glittery aqua-colored gift bag to Sienna. It was mine!

I stepped away from Finn a bit; I wanted to make sure I was in the shot, *without* him. This moment was all about sister power.

She opened the bag and took out an oversized navy-blue shirt.

"Oh...wow. A—a youth center shirt? I mean, this is great! Thanks, Mia. I always need...pajamas," she said awkwardly.

I giggled. "Keep going."

She looked confused. Next she pulled out a matching baseball cap.

"A hat?" Sienna asked. "What's going on, Mia?"

"You're not done," I told her excitedly.

She looked at Mom, who shrugged. Then, Sienna reached in and pulled out the brochure.

"A brochure? For..." the more she read, the more her eyes widened and her jaw dropped.

Bingo! Now *this* was the reaction I was looking for!

"*Space camp?!*" she shrieked. "Mia! This is incredible! Two days at the youth center, meeting real astronauts—I get to eat space food! Oh, my gosh! And do zero gravity! I can't believe this!"

I laughed. "Do you like it?"

"Are you kidding me?" Sienna jumped off the high stool she'd been sitting on and ran to me, throwing her arms around me. "It's only the best birthday present in the history of birthday presents! Thank you, thank you, thank you. I love it."

"I'm so glad," I told her. "I just wanted to make your ninth birthday special."

"You did," she told me. "You really, really did!"

As her friends gathered around her to congratulate her and *ooh* and *aah* over the space camp brochure, I fell back a bit. All of that worrying, and I'd done it—nailed the perfect present for my sister. She was going to have the time of her life at space camp. It was worth every weird and stressful thing I'd had to do. Sienna had really helped me with *Mia's Life* and pushed me to get out of my comfort zone when she knew I needed it. She deserved to have a phenomenal time at space camp and an awesome birthday party.

Briony gave me a hug. "You killed it, Mia! She loves it."

"She does, doesn't she?" I said, beaming.

"It was such a great idea," Finn said. "Your sister's really into space, huh?"

"Um, did you see the party?" laughed Briony as she motioned around.

I grinned at Finn. "I guess you two haven't properly met. Finn, Briony. Briony...Rock-Climbing Boy."

Finn smirked. "Please—I know who you are. The girl who loves soft pretzels and always orders a Frappuccino at Starbucks."

"Someone's been watching *Mia's Life*," sang Briony.

"Well, I had to, once I met the real live star," Finn said, flashing me a smile. Would that smile ever get old? I didn't think so!

"Who wants cake?" called out Dad.

"*Me!*" practically everyone in the yard shouted.

"Come on," I said with a laugh, "let's eat!"

The birthday party continued on the entire afternoon. Finally, everyone had left, and it was just me and my family, cozied up in our pajamas in the living room. We'd decided to leave the mess and deal with it tomorrow, which we'd probably regret, but who cared?

Before Finn had taken off, we'd made plans to meet up again. I was really excited to get to know him better, and I kept taking out my phone and staring at his name in my contacts. It reminded me of when I'd pranked Sienna by hanging pictures of her crush all over her bedroom walls—good thing she didn't have a photo of Finn!

"Well, Sienna?" Mom asked. "Did you have a good birthday?"

"Best. Birthday. *Ever*," she said with a sleepy smile.

"I'm so glad," Dad said. "We're thankful for you, and we hope that your party made you as happy as you make us."

"Aww. I love you guys," said Sienna.

"Wuv you!" Karma said, giving Sienna a super loud kiss on the cheek, which made us all crack up.

"All right, nine-year-old. Time for bed. And these little ones too. You going to hit the hay soon, Mia?" Mom asked.

"I think I'm going to make a video first, actually," I said.

"A video?" Dad asked. "We've been filming all day!"

"Not for the vlog, I think. A quick one on Instagram," I said. "Just...something informal. I'll post the one for the party tomorrow."

"All right. Just don't stay up too late. It was a big day for all of us," Mom said.

"Good night," I told the rest of my family before disappearing into my bedroom.

As I sat at my desk, I looked at the photo next to my computer. It was me and Sienna, with our cheeks squished together. Our hair was tangled together, and we just looked so *happy*. Happy to be cheering each other on and learning more and more every day.

There were a million Siennas out there watching me. And I owed them a big thank-you.

I got cozy in my favorite corner of my room, on a bright multicolored cushion, before picking up my phone, opening up an Instagram Live, and hitting *record*.

"Well...this is it," I said. "Sienna's birthday is over. I can't believe it." I tried not to read the comments as they flooded in quickly. There were lots of heart emojis and *HI MIA*s.

"I guess I really just wanted to come on here and give a huge thank-you to all of the Miacorns," I said. "This week has been incredible. It's led to me trying so many new things that I was pretty afraid of doing. I learned how to be confident: I know that I can do things that might seem really scary, but that if I put myself out there, something better than I ever could have imagined might happen. I discovered a new hobby, made a new friend, and found Sienna the absolute *perfect* present. You guys will see all of the details and the big reveal tomorrow, but...thank you." I took a deep breath and continued.

"So often, people tell me that I inspire them. Because I've made a coloring book, or because I've been able to travel the world, or because I have such a tight relationship with my family. But the truth is, you Miacorns inspire *me*. When I was feeling insecure, you pushed me to try new things. You all were brave when I wasn't. And I can't thank you enough for that. So, thank you. Thank you for watching my videos. Thank you for being part of my life. And last but not least, thank you for introducing me to my newest love..." I paused for dramatic effect. "Rock climbing, obvi! What did you think I was going to say?" And, with a wink, I clicked off the video.

Mia's Life
1.02M subscribers

Just as I was crawling into bed, there was a knock on my door.

"Mia?" There was Sienna, in her hot-pink pajamas.

"Hey, Sienna. Shouldn't you be heading to bed?"

"In a second." She came in and sat on my bed. I scooted over to make room and she flopped onto my pillows.

"Hey," I laughed. "Scooch."

"I wanted to say thanks again for my present. I'm really, really excited, and it was my favorite thing I got all day."

I shook my head. "Sienna, I should be thanking you. Without you, I never would have given *Mia's Life* the shake-up it needed. I got a huge confidence boost this week, and I know a lot of it was thanks to my not-so-little-anymore sister."

She grinned. "And don't forget... Without me, you wouldn't have met Finn."

"Yeah, yeah! Now, out of here. I need to sleep."

"Love you, Mia."

"Love you, Sienna."

As my sister left and shut the door behind her, I fell back onto my pillow, my head finding the exact spot hers had been in. And as my eyes slowly closed and night pulled me toward sleep, I knew I'd dream about how amazing the day had been.

Because *Mia's Life* was great.

But Mia's life?

Even better.

ABOUT THE AUTHOR

Mia Fizz is a fifteen-year-old social media star with more than one million subscribers on her YouTube channel (*Mia's Life*). She's been featured in numerous magazines, has written multiple Amazon-bestselling books, and has appeared in a sold-out live show alongside her family. When not featuring on her family's YouTube channel (*Family Fizz*, which has more than two million subscribers), she likes to cook, practice Spanish, rock climb, and draw.